PLAYTIME RHYMES

For Judith
with all my love

Book design by Tracey Cunnell

First published in Great Britain in 1995
by Orion Children's Books
a division of the Orion Publishing Group Ltd
Orion House
5 Upper St Martin's Lane
London   WC2H 9EA

PLAYTIME RHYMES

Illustrated by Sally Gardner

Orion
Children's Books

CONTENTS

Down by the station

Down by the station, early in the morning,
See the little puffer trains all in a row.
See the engine driver pull the little handle.
Choo, choo, choo, and off we go.

Down at the farmyard, early in the morning,
See the little tractor standing in the barn.
Do you see the farmer pull the little handle?
Chug, chug, chug, and off we go.

If you're happy and you know it

If you're happy and you know it, clap your hands;
If you're happy and you know it, clap your hands;
If you're happy and you know it,
And you really want to show it,
If you're happy and you know it, clap your hands!

You can add more verses like this:

If you're happy and you know it, stamp your feet

If you're happy and you know it, nod your head

If you're happy and you know it, wave your hand

If you're happy and you know it, shout "We are!"

Ten fat sausages

Ten fat sausages sizzling in the pan,
One went **POP!** and another went *BANG!*

Eight fat sausages sizzling in the pan,
One went **POP!** and another went *BANG!*

Six fat sausages sizzling in the pan,
One went **POP!** and another went *BANG!*

Four fat sausages sizzling in the pan,
One went **POP!** and another went *BANG!*

Two fat sausages sizzling in the pan,
One went **POP!** and another went *BANG!*

No fat sausages sizzling in the pan,
But, all of a sudden, the pan went *BANG!*

It went *BANG!* It went *BANG!*

It went *BANG! BANG! BANG!*

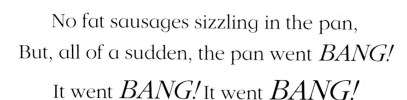

Now there are no sizzling sausages
And no frying pan!

Ten fat peas

Ten fat peas in a
pea-pod pressed,
one grew,
two grew
and so did all the rest;
they grew,
and they grew,
and did not stop
until one day
the pod went
POP!

15

Dinosaur soup

Listen to the chorus of the brontosaurus
And the stegosaurus down by the swamp.
Along comes a dinosaur, making such a loud roar,
Thumping with his feet and going stomp, stomp, stomp.

Pterodactyl flapping, long beak clacking,
Big teeth snapping, down from the tree.
Here's the woolly mammoth, tusks all curly,
Joins the hurly-burly, oh dear me!

What a noise, it's the boys
Of the prehistoric animal brigade.
What a noise, it's the boys
Of the prehistoric animal brigade.

I hear thunder

I hear thunder, I hear thunder.
Hark, don't you? Hark, don't you?
Pitter-patter raindrops,
Pitter-patter raindrops,
I'm wet through,
So are you!

I see blue skies, I see blue skies
Way up high, way up high;
Hurry up the sunshine,
Hurry up the sunshine,
We'll soon dry,
We'll soon dry!

Pat-a-cake

Pat-a-cake, pat-a-cake, baker's man,
Bake me a cake as fast as you can;
Pat it and prick it and mark it with B,
And put it in the oven for baby and me.

I'm a little teapot

I'm a little teapot, short and stout,
Here's my handle, here's my spout.
When I get the steam up, hear me shout,
"Tip me up and pour me out."

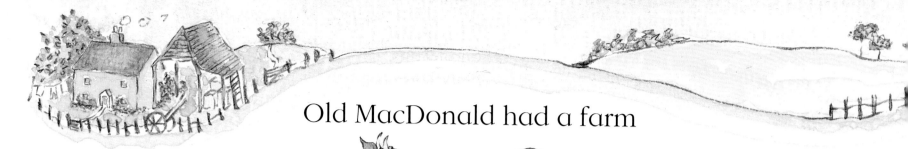

Old MacDonald had a farm

Old MacDonald had a farm,
E - I - E - I - O !
And on that farm he had some cows,
E - I - E - I - O !

With a *moo-moo* here, and a *moo-moo* there,
Here a *moo*, there a *moo*,
Everywhere a *moo-moo*!
Old MacDonald had a farm,
E - I - E - I - O !

Old MacDonald had a farm,
E - I - E - I - O !
And on that farm he had some ducks,
E - I - E - I - O !

With a *quack-quack* here, and a *quack-quack* there,
Here a *quack*, there a *quack*,
Everywhere a *quack-quack*!
Old MacDonald had a farm,
E - I - E - I - O !

Old MacDonald had a farm,

E - I - E - I - O !

And on that farm he had some sheep,

E - I - E - I - O !

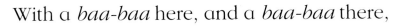

With a *baa-baa* here, and a *baa-baa* there,

Here a *baa*, there a *baa*,

Everywhere a *baa-baa*!

Old MacDonald had a farm,

E - I - E - I - O !

Old MacDonald had a farm,

E - I - E - I - O !

And on that farm he had some pigs,

E - I - E - I - O !

With an *oink-oink* here, and an *oink-oink* there,

Here an *oink*, there an *oink*,

Everywhere an *oink-oink*!

Old MacDonald had a farm,

E - I - E - I - O !

You can add more verses to this for horses, dogs and cats.

21

Ten in the bed

There were ten in the bed,
And the little one said,
"Roll over! Roll over!"
So they all rolled over
And one fell out.
He gave a little scream—"OW!"
He gave a little shout—"HEY!"

22

Carry on like this to the end with

five

four

three

two

nine

eight

seven

six

and then...

There was one in the bed,
The little one, who said,

"GOODNIGHT!"

23

This little pig

This little pig went to market, this little pig stayed at home,

This little pig had roast beef, this little pig had none,

And this little pig cried, *"Wee-wee-wee-wee-wee,"* all the way home.

Ten little fingers

I have ten little fingers,
And they all belong to me.
I can make them do things.
Would you like to see?

I can shut them up tight,
Or open them all wide.
I can put them all together,
Or make them all hide.

I can make them jump high,
I can make them jump low.
I can fold them quietly,
And sit just so.

The wheels on the bus

The wheels on the bus go round and round,
Round and round, round and round;
The wheels on the bus go round and round,
All day long.

You can add lots more verses like this:

The doors on the bus go open and shut

The horn on the bus goes beep! beep! beep!

The wipers on the bus go swish! swish! swish!

The driver on the bus says, "Move along, please!"

The children on the bus go bumpety bump

The mummies on the bus go, "Chat! Chat! Chat!"

The daddies on the bus go nod, nod, nod

The babies on the bus cry, "WAAH! WAAH! WAAH!"

The doggies on the bus bark, "Woof! Woof! Woof!"

Ring-a-ring o'roses

Ring-a-ring o'roses,
A pocket full of posies;
Atishoo! Atishoo!
We all fall down!

Roly poly

Roly poly, roly poly, up, up, up;
Roly poly, roly poly, down, down, down;
Roly poly, roly poly, out, out, out;
Roly poly, roly poly, in, in, in.

Roly poly, ever so slowly...ever...so...slowly.
Roly poly, faster, faster, FASTER, FASTER!

Incy Wincy Spider

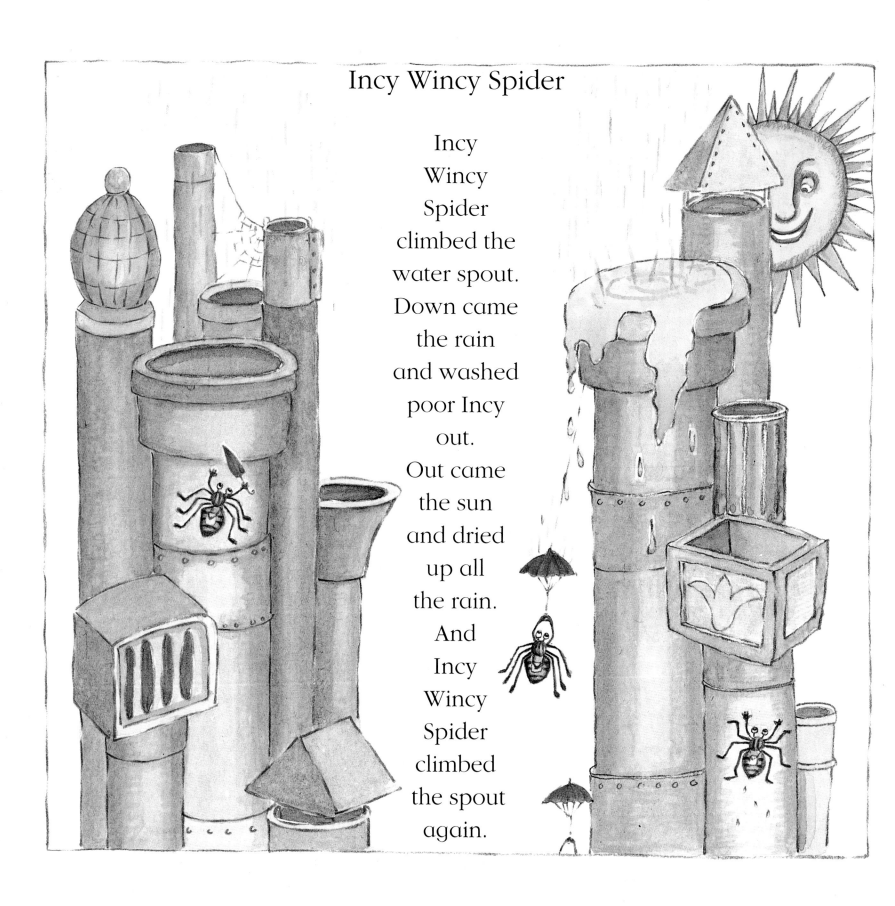

Incy
Wincy
Spider
climbed the
water spout.
Down came
the rain
and washed
poor Incy
out.
Out came
the sun
and dried
up all
the rain.
And
Incy
Wincy
Spider
climbed
the spout
again.

Round and round the garden

Round and round the garden
Like a teddy bear;
One step, two steps,
Tickly under there.

The farmer's in his dell

The farmer's in his dell,
The farmer's in his dell,
E...I...E...I
The farmer's in his dell.

The farmer picks a wife,
The farmer picks a wife,
E...I...E...I
The farmer picks a wife.

32

Sing the other verses like this:

The wife picks a child

The child picks a nurse

The nurse picks a dog

We all pat the dog

33

My hands

My hands upon my head I place, on my shoulders, on my face;

On my hips I place them—so, then bend down to touch my toe.

Now I raise them up so high, make my fingers fairly fly;

Now I clap them, one, two, three. Then I fold them silently.

Here we go round the mulberry bush

Here we go round the mulberry bush,
The mulberry bush, the mulberry bush,
Here we go round the mulberry bush
On a cold and frosty morning.

This is the way we sweep the floor,
Sweep the floor, sweep the floor,
This is the way we sweep the floor
On a cold and frosty morning.

This is the way we scrub our clothes,
Scrub our clothes, scrub our clothes,
This is the way we scrub our clothes
On a cold and frosty morning.

Miss Polly had a dolly

Miss Polly had a dolly who was sick, sick, sick.

So she called for the doctor to be quick, quick, quick.

The doctor came with his bag and his hat,

And he knocked on the door with a rat-a-tat-tat.

He looked at the dolly, and he shook his head,

And he said, "Miss Polly, put her straight to bed."

He wrote on a paper for a pill, pill, pill.

"That will make her better, yes it will, will, will!"

This is the way the ladies ride

This is the way the ladies ride,
Trippetty-tee!
Trippetty-tee!
This is the way the ladies ride,
Trippetty-trippetty-tee!

This is the way the gentlemen ride,
Gallopy-gallop!
Gallopy-gallop!
This is the way the gentlemen ride,
Gallopy-gallopy-gallop!

This is the way the farmers ride,
Jiggetty-jog!
Jiggetty-jog!
This is the way the farmers ride,
Jiggetty-jiggetty-jog!
And

    D-O-W-N

        into

           the

             ditch.

Looby Lou

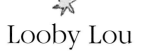

Here we go Looby Lou,
Here we go Looby Light,
Here we go Looby Lou,
All on a Saturday night.

You put your right foot in,
You put your right foot out,
You shake it a little, a little,
And turn yourself about.

You can add more verses like this:

You put your left foot in

You put your right hand in

You put your left hand in

You put your whole self in

The beehive

Here is the beehive.

Where are the bees?

Hidden away where nobody sees.

Watch as they come out of their hive—

One, two, three, four, five!

An elephant

An elephant goes like this and that,
He's terribly big,
And he's terribly fat;
He has no fingers,
And he has no toes,
But goodness gracious,
What a long nose!

Tommy Thumb

Tommy Thumb, Tommy Thumb, where are you?
Here I am, here I am, how do you do?

Peter Pointer, Peter Pointer, where are you?
Here I am, here I am, how do you do?

Middle Man, Middle Man, where are you?
Here I am, here I am, how do you do?

Ruby Ring, Ruby Ring, where are you?
Here I am, here I am, how do you do?

Baby Small, Baby Small, where are you?
Here I am, here I am, how do you do?

Fingers all, fingers all, where are you?
Here we are, here we are, how do you do?

One, two, three, four, five

One, two, three, four, five,
Once I caught a fish alive;

Six, seven, eight, nine, ten,
Then I let him go again.

Why did you let him go?
Because he bit my finger so!

Which finger did he bite?
This little finger on the right!

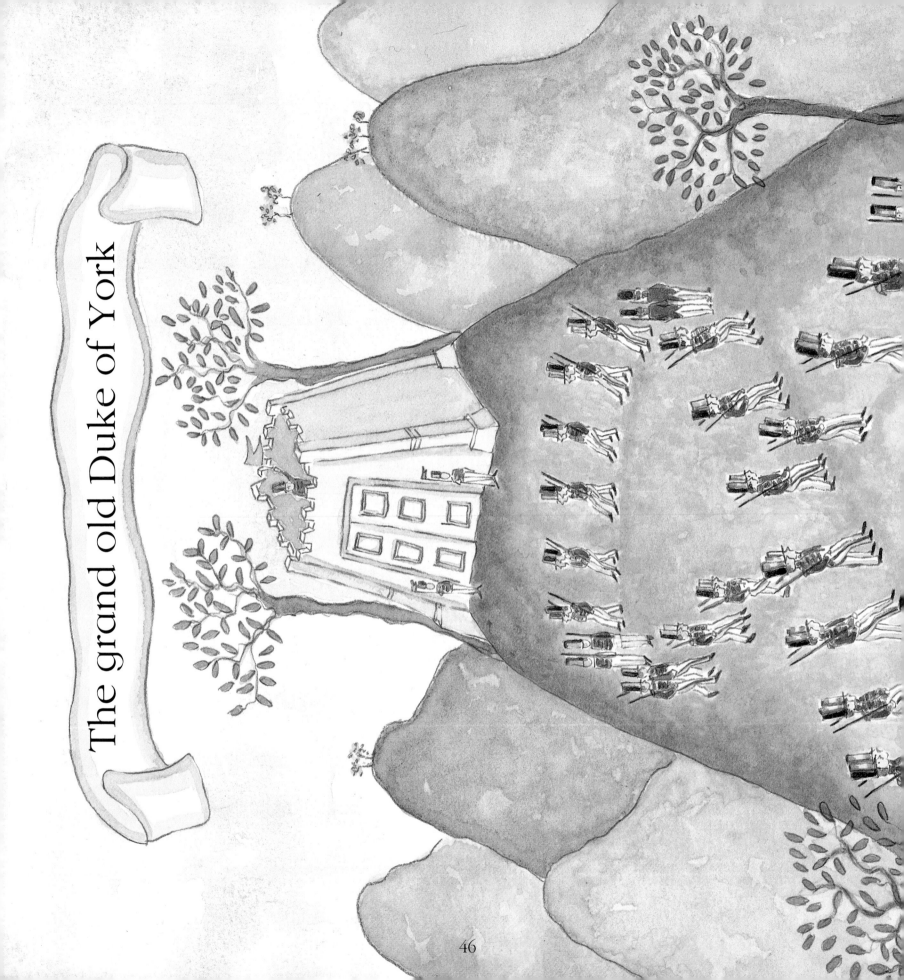

The grand old Duke of York

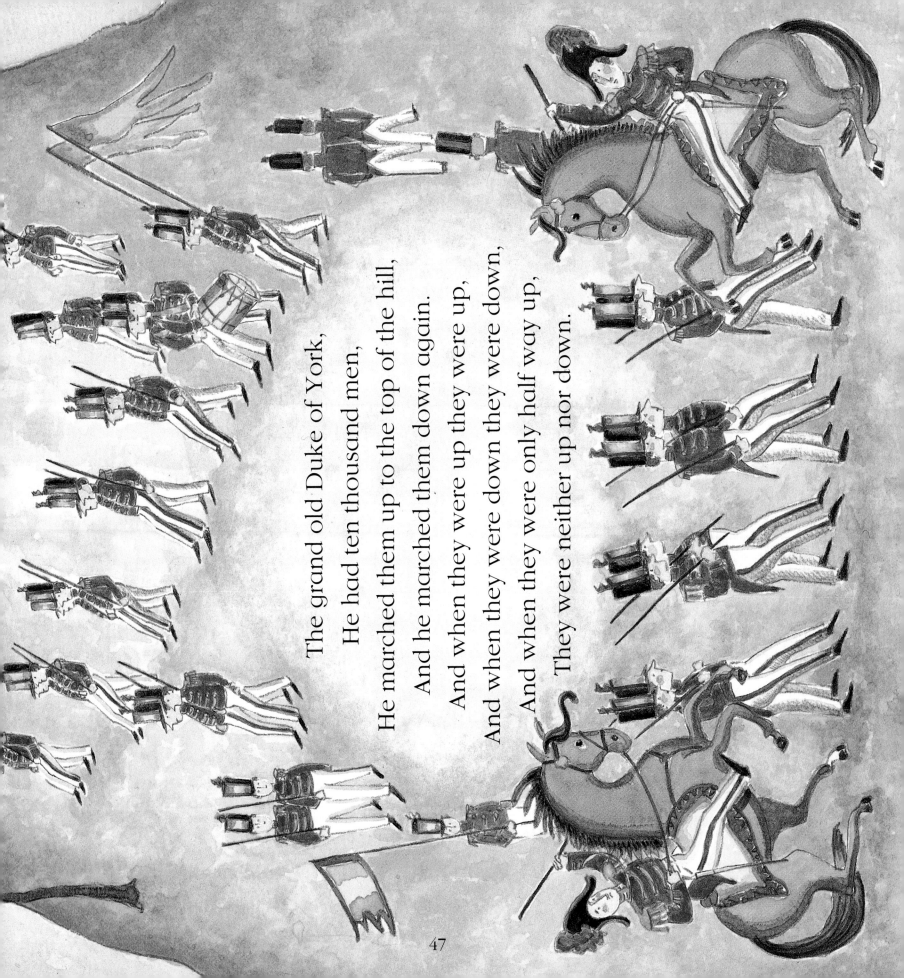

The grand old Duke of York,
He had ten thousand men,
He marched them up to the top of the hill,
And he marched them down again.
And when they were up they were up,
And when they were down they were down,
And when they were only half way up,
They were neither up nor down.

Dance to your daddy

Dance to your daddy,
My bonny laddy,
Dance to your daddy,
My little lamb.

You shall have a fishy,
In a little dishy,
You shall have a fishy,
When the boat comes in.

Dance to your daddy,
My bonny laddy,
Dance to your daddy,
My little lamb.

48

Here is the church

Here is the church,
Here is the steeple,
Open the doors
And here are the people.
Here's the parson going upstairs,
And here he is a-saying his prayers.

Three little monkeys

Three little monkeys were jumping on the bed,
One fell off and bumped her head;
Her mummy called the doctor
And the doctor said,
"No more jumping on the bed!"

Two little monkeys were jumping on the bed,
One fell off and bumped his head;
His mummy called the doctor
And the doctor said,
"Do keep those monkeys off that bed!"

One little monkey was jumping on the bed,
She fell off and bumped her head;
Her mummy called the doctor
And the doctor said,
"Well, that's what you get for jumping on the bed!"

Six little mice

Six little mice sat down to spin,
Pussy passed by and she peeped in:
What are you at, my little men?
We're making coats for gentlemen.
Shall I come in and cut your threads?
No, no, Pussy, you'd bite off our heads.

Two little dicky-birds

Two little dicky-birds, sitting on a wall;

One named Peter, one named Paul.

Fly away, Peter! Fly away, Paul!

Come back, Peter! Come back, Paul!

Five little ducks

Five little ducks went swimming one day,
Over the pond and far away.
Mother Duck said, "Quack, quack, quack, quack,"
But only four little ducks came back.

Four little ducks went swimming one day,
Over the pond and far away.
Mother Duck said, "Quack, quack, quack, quack,"
But only three little ducks came back.

Three little ducks went swimming one day,
Over the pond and far away.
Mother Duck said, "Quack, quack, quack, quack,"
But only two little ducks came back.

Two little ducks went swimming one day,

Over the pond and far away.

Mother Duck said, "Quack, quack, quack, quack,"

But only one little duck came back.

One little duck went swimming one day,

Over the pond and far away.

Mother Duck said, "Quack, quack, quack, quack,"

And five little ducks came swimming back.

Teddy bear, teddy bear

Teddy bear, teddy bear, touch your nose,

Teddy bear, teddy bear, touch your toes;

Teddy bear, teddy bear, touch the ground,

Teddy bear, teddy bear, turn around.

Teddy bear, teddy bear, climb the stairs,

Teddy bear, teddy bear, say your prayers;

Teddy bear, teddy bear, turn off the light,

Teddy bear, teddy bear, say goodnight!

Twinkle, twinkle, little star

Twinkle, twinkle, little star,
How I wonder what you are!
Up above the world so high,
Like a diamond in the sky.
Twinkle, twinkle, little star,
How I wonder what you are.

The ostrich

Here is the ostrich, straight and tall,
Nodding his head above us all.
Here is the hedgehog, prickly and small,
Rolling himself into a ball.
Here is the spider, scuttling around,
Treading so lightly on the ground.
Here are the birds that fly so high,
Spreading their wings across the sky.
Here are the children, fast asleep,
And in the night the owls do peep,
Too-whit, too-woo, too-whit, too-woo.

INDEX OF FIRST LINES